Common Ground

Anyone?

Rhyme Time for SW Mums

by
Sarah Clarke-Wareham

authorHOUSE®

AuthorHouse™ UK Ltd.
500 Avebury Boulevard
Central Milton Keynes, MK9 2BE
www.authorhouse.co.uk
Phone: 08001974150

First published by AuthorHouse 12/18/2009

ISBN: 978-1-4490-5189-1 (sc)

This book is printed on acid-free paper.

And you thought I just wanted your friendship....

Thanks to everyone who has unwittingly given me the richest,
most hilarious and forever comforting content for these poems

The list is endless but particularly to Becky, Bex, Nicky, Sarah S, Selina,
Marie-Claire, Charts, Sarah H, Emma, Alex, Sarah Twins, Amanda, Justine, Emily,
Chantal, Angela, Abby, Sarah C, Jo, Anna, Tash, Liz
and of course my own (fantastic) mum

And an even bigger thank you to those children
who created all that mischief in the first place

To my children Scarlett & Finn, their cousins Lily, Millie and the Max's, and to Oli, Sam,
Alice, Freddie, Belle, the Amelia's, the Ben's, the Jack's, Toby, Bella, Ava, Amy, Oscar,
George, Charlie, Max, Audrey, Evelyn, Joe, Sofia, Violet, Frankie....

And a final thank you to Chris; for pretending to enjoy poems
written entirely for women, and laughing in all the right places.

Common Ground

Rhyme Time for
SW Mums

by
Sarah Clarke-Wareham

Oh what a tangled web we weave
When we practice to conceive...

Weight a while longer?

"Y'know you're the fattest girl I've ever slept with" husband makes the revelation
"Well I am 8 months pregnant" you retort. "You do the equation"
But secretly you worry, because you don't much resemble his bride
Your toes in constant shadow, your bottom twice as wide
You wonder if it's normal in pregnancy to reach a size 16
If bingo wings and tree trunk thighs are essential for the Mummy scene
But you don't want to spoil the occasion so you put on a positive front
Until mother-in-law says in the post natal ward, "Gosh you still look 5 months pregnant!"

You jump on the scales; do the maths, "NO! There must be some mistake!"
Placenta weighed about 2 pounds, and Charlie was well over 8!
    (So why the hell haven't I lost more weight??)
9 months on, 9 months off, the midwife reminds you with patronising calm
But you have 3 weddings and Ascot this summer, so that causes some alarm
"Breastfeeding will be my saviour, you think, it'll shift those pounds no probs"
But all it really seems to shift is another packet of chocolate Hob Nobs
You mix dieting with healthy eating, intermittent with frenzied snacking
Failed attempts to get in those 7 jeans suggests the regime may be lacking
So you conclude with some reluctance, as you munch on the kid's cold fries
The only way to get your figure back is to do some exercise

First you try Buggy Fit in the park, but you just can't stick at that
Frankly running around the common with a pram makes you feel a bit of a .....
    (Sometimes it's just better to stay fat)
You spot British Military Fitness on your jogs, perhaps that's more your type of thing
But sweaty men barking orders? Never going to be more than a passing fling
You shell out for a Personal Trainer. He's gorgeous and makes you feel great
Until some wee-wee escapes during sprinting, and you cancel all future dates
So what's the verdict? Are you going to be forever in that empire line dress?
Not according to those posters, as you sign up to Fit for a Princess

But the summer's not what you'd hoped for, and you don't do exercise in the rain
Plus wearing Lycra in public goes a little against the grain
But you don't want friends and family to see this as just a passing whim
So you put his credit card to work again, and join Canons Gym
     (Okay, Nuffield Health, but it doesn't have quite the same ring)
You can't put your finger on why it's so good, why you go without persuasion
Is it the shiny machines, vast rows of weights or South Africans with chests all shaven?
Is it the variety of aerobic classes or how they serve their smoothies fresh?
Or is it actually just the gossip, manicures and their ever popular crèche...

But times are hard and £70 a month on coffee mornings is a little steep
And what's the point of paying for crèche while they're having their morning sleep?
     (Surely that's time better spent shopping on Clapham High St?)
So a change of tack and another trip to Sweaty Betty is required
You plan to go running every night (unless of course you're too tired)
     When the nanny points out that's every night, you point out she's fired
Finally you make it out one sultry eve, and actually it's quite a thrill
Girls Aloud do you proud as you huff and puff up the hill
A builder's wolf whistle makes you feel good; a Granny running past you does not
You hear the ch-chink of al fresco drinking and wonder if you should stop
But you keep your focus, head for home, your 5k goal in sight
Day dreaming of all the food you're going to eat for the rest of the night
     (After all, Lycra is meant to be tight....)

It seems that you eat when you're bored, exercise, and then eat again
In fact the real mystery is how you ever managed to be a neat size 10
How do you retain a gorgeous body, without making a sacrifice?
How can you have a hectic social life and still remain the trophy wife?
There's nothing for it, you admit with a sigh, except to have another child
It may not make you slim again, but at least it puts the problem off for a while

School talk rules?
Or fools talk schools?

Old men talk about the war, old ladies about the weather
All men talk about football, while teenagers discuss "whatever"
Young girls talk about boys, make-up, fashion and shoes
But Mums? What do Mum's talk about? Of course, we talk schools!

In the minority are the organised Mums who have it sorted from the off
"Urmm name down at Finton, Thomas's, and Broomwood..." they admit with a nervous
    cough
Of course head teachers can spot this type from a hundred miles away
An extra homemade cake adorns their plate, when they visit on Open Day

And then there is the "unaware Mum", an even rarer breed
"Well, they're only three" they mumble, with a growing unease
"Indeed" you respond reassuringly, hardly containing your glee
If they haven't thought about schools, well, that's one more place for me

And then there is the vast majority of Mum's in South West London
To whom schools is a constant source of worry, a regular conundrum
We talk about it in coffee shops while administering Babyccino
We discover neighbours without a place at all, which comes as a bit of a blow
"Luckily we're 2 doors from Honeywell" a Mum declares sounding slightly smug
As you wonder how much damage can be caused by a Starbucks Grande mug
"We've got a place at Putney High" you say, while wondering why you've lied
Until your conversation is interrupted by "Love, is that your kid just run outside?"

So you take the discussion home, after all, you share the parental role
But by option 3 you see they're getting bored, fumbling for the remote control
"Darling" they smile disarmingly "I'm so grateful for all your hard work
If I tried to butt in now, I'd end up sounding like a jerk
I'm sure whatever school you choose will be the bee's knees"
While you wonder if they'll be quite so pleased when they see the school fees

And so the decision is left to you and you really start to panic
You liken a place at the local school to the sinking of the titanic
You phone around the private schools, "Sorry, absolutely no places I'm afraid"
You think about High School entrance exams but worry they won't make the grade
    (As you watch them trying to eat baked beans with a spade)
You consider being sneaky, renting a one bed flat by Beatrix Potter
But start to dream of council officials with handcuffs, screaming "I've got her!"

You consider a move to the countryside, green spaces and picket fences
But a few visits to Suburbia soon pull you to your senses
You wonder about scholarships, Timmy's swimming came on so well in France
But apparently, at 4, they don't extend "potential" to hard cash grants
At coffee one morning, a mother suggests home schooling, which creates quite a roar
And while you join the other mum's in laughter, you mentally log it under "final straw"

And so you enter the final furlong without a solid plan
The 21st March arrives; you hyperventilate as you spot the postman
You open the letter with despondent hands, is the local school too bad to bear?
A moment later and: "Bloody hell! She hasn't got a place anywhere!"
But when all seems lost, you hate the world, your husband suggests you're not at your
    nicest
You get that call from Finton House. Thank GOD for the CREDIT CRISIS!

The price of threedom

While schools will always be high on our agenda, there is another subject we debate
And frankly one that needs a decision, before our body clocks deem it too late
We discuss the pros & cons at length, and largely all agree
Having 2 kids is a nightmare. So let's have number 3.

First there is the "born to be a..." Mum, who procreates with style
To her having 3 under 3 doesn't appear the slightest bit of a trial
A conveyor belt for nappy changes, a buggy with a wide load sticker
The baby acting as a buffer, when the toddlers start to bicker
More hours spent feeding than sleeping, mere survival a beautiful thing
In fact, it's amazing what some Mums will do to get their eternity ring!

Next there is the "Mum of Boys". She can't help it. She wants a girl
Odds are stacked against her, but she's giving it a whirl
We spend 9 months guessing, using a purely "scientific approach"
Pulse rate, body shape, conception date, even leg hair growth
But finally the day of reckoning, will it be pink fluff or a rugby team?
Funnily enough, no one cares anymore. "It's a baby!" we all scream
     (We still haven't quite got the inevitability of that, it would seem)

And hard to believe in 2009, but there is still the accident prone Mum
Relying on that breastfeeding myth, but there's another reason her period doesn't come
The thought of having 3 pre-schoolers comes as a bit of a shock
While husband's concerns are more post-school, and paying for his growing flock
But not every accident is accidental. Cue: share a knowing smile
Because there's little you can do to stop her, when a woman wants a child

Next there is the delusional Mum who is perfectly happy with two
But 3 appears to be the magic number, so what else can she do?
There must be something in it, she thinks, as another friend whispers her news
Although it's hard to see the positive of a further 9 months off booze
Husband worries it's a status thing, do people think we can't afford more?
Decision quickly made then and it's "Darling, we're having four"

And then there are the rest of us, what I call the "irrational Mum"
Revelling in our new found freedom, but thinking "Y'know, I'm just not done"
We don't look forward to pregnancy followed by hours of excruciating pain
Months of sleep deprivation, that mushy new Mum brain
We're not keen on middle child syndrome, gorgeous Tommy suddenly not so sweet
But we deem these steps acceptable, to make our family complete

The first obstacle in our way is the size of our home -
Problem easily resolved though as we get Absolute Lofts on the phone
Next we need to change the car; the Audi Estate suddenly looks too small
We quickly choose a seven seater, more room for the kids to brawl
And of course we pre-book childcare, not keen on a 3 to 1 ratio
Although fully expecting the nanny to take on the complete trio

So all preparations are completed, but something just doesn't feel right
Such military planning implemented, surely you haven't made an oversight?
Ah of course! You forgot to tell the husband; well it's an easy mistake to make
Best not disturb him right now, as you give the pregnancy test a shake...

They are what they eat: sweet

It seemed a little strange back then, when you'd watch their eyes glaze over
And all because you'd asked for a second helping of their Pavlova
How they'd watch you eat each mouthful with undisguised delight
A clear plate after Sunday Roast, to them a perfect sight
How they'd visit you at Uni but to your student antics, wouldn't listen
Too busy filling cupboards, caring only for your nutrition
And now in your mid thirties, they're still obsessed with filling your tum
But suddenly it doesn't seem so strange, now you've become a Mum

6 months arrives, time for weaning (don't tell anyone you started at 4)
Baby rice swiftly rejected, so it's vegetables galore
    (Although to be fair, most ends up on the floor)
We steam, blend, puree, mash, organic peas we shell
Suddenly we can't serve broccoli without the help of Annabel Karmel
We only buy from the local farmer's market – well, at least until Number 2
Novelty's worn off by then; Sainsbury's basics will have to do
We invest in extensive plastic protection, but the ceiling still needs a wash
Husband wonders quietly why his ice tray is full of butternut squash
So logically we should hate this time, as more sweet potato goes SPLAT
But watching your child be nourished? It doesn't get much better than that.

And so they grow, and with them the range of food they refuse to eat
When Organix "Carrot Sticks" are their only vegetable, you realise it's time to cheat
You try the Charlie & Lola tactic "Darling, these are Greenland drops, not peas"
But they look at you disdainfully, so you resort to covering them in cheese
You wonder if their 5 a day can consist purely of fruitpot and raisin
You stick them in front of Lazytown, hoping Sportacus can bring a health food craze on
But finally, every ingenious plan exhausted, you realise it's all a farce
So you throw the towel in, hold back tears, and bribe them with chocolate stars

Of course you regularly take them out for meals; after all you're an SW Mum
Husband may be having a tricky time at work, but you're the long suffering one
So it's Crumpet at lunchtime followed by tea at Pizza Express
A glass of wine for you, while someone else clears up the mess
You train the kids to keep these restaurant outings from their Dad
But then another pack of Carluccios crayons falls out of your handbag
> ("Darling, I know you've lost £100 million this year, but there's really no need to nag")

And then one day, that fatal error – you take them out of SW18
To a restaurant with linen tablecloths, and a passing interest in keeping them clean
Where adults outnumber children, my, what a strange sight that is
You cajole, scold, plead, and bribe while sinking lower into your glass of fizz
You try to ignore those dagger stares as Toby escapes from your grasp once more
Zig zagging through the restaurant, narrowly missing contact with the kitchen door
Complimentary bread consumed, hugely priced roast lamb stays on the plate
You call for the bill, leave a 20% tip and file the experience under "BIG mistake"

And so your love/ hate relationship with meal time continues
Your fish pie rejected and you instantly blow a fuse
But a finished plate, or dare I say it, a "Thank you, that was yum!"
Really is one of the sweetest things you experience as a Mum
You may never be Tana Ramsay, or avoid preservatives altogether
You may wonder (guiltily) if fish oils really make kids clever
It may always seem that yours lurch from one food fad to another
While there will always be that kid munching carrot, and of course his smug mother
But as we search frantically, for the slightest positive to grope
There is, at least, some good news that gives us room for hope
Something you might call progress, if you felt the urge to gloat
At least they don't live off Angel Delight and cola ice cream float
> (Do you remember those days? They still get my vote!)

It's a One Woman Show

Before we had kids, weren't we proud of our ability to multi-task?
Laugh at men who found doing 2 things at once way beyond their grasp
But then we became Mum's and realised what a dirty great hole we'd dug
"Oooh we can do lots of things!" Only now, not so smug

Role Number 1: Head Domestic, Main responsibilities include:
Menu planning, cooking with love, and then throwing away most of the food
Washing, drying, and ironing. Putting away freshly folded pants
Wondering if men still believe in fairies; and that's why they don't say thanks.
Tidying the house five times a day, cleaning (when the cleaner's off sick)
Desperately spraying Mr Muscle, as George gives the floor another lick
You do get help from time to time, but at 4, they're more of a hindrance
And how much do you earn for this varied role? Well, less than thruppence

Role Number 2: Social Secretary, multiple diaries to synchronize
Amelia seems to feature heavily, considering her relative size
Birthday parties, play dates. Of course Playball, Ballet & Gym
Poor Harry had his own play date once... but that was just a whim
There are weekends with the grandparents, or those usurpers who've left the city
Military planned packing required, to forget Blankie would be a pity (to say the least)
Husband's diary needs micro-management, often known to double book
Well, beers with the boys is more fun than parent's evening, so it's worth taking a look
"If it wasn't for me" you grumble "as a couple we'd have no social life!
He's YOUR best friend after all, so why am I discussing diaries with his wife?"
But you do it all, from dates to restaurants and booking the baby sitter
Husband seems unable to communicate, despite spending hours on Twitter

Role number 3: Event Co-ordinator. No experience but you're giving it a go
Father Christmas is loved by all, but you reckon its Mary who's running the show
No man could start planning in October, focus on preparing the Master List
Appreciate how much effort goes into those 3 days of getting p*ssed
He wouldn't know Lisa's dress size, or the age of every niece
The far reaching effects innocent overspend can have on family peace
So you plan, shop, write and wrap while husband entertains clients
At least he understands that diamonds are the only way to guarantee compliance
But of course Christmas isn't the only event you have to organise each year
Three holidays may be nice, but they don't just magically appear
At least this is a role that pays you, if not in cash, then in kind
Although not getting time off from your other jobs means it slightly loses its shine...

Role number 4 you try to avoid as it's usually during unsociable hours
Surely Friday night should be bath & book, not exerting your sexual prowess?
You seem to spend more time preparing for sex than you do performing the act
Shaving, waxing, plucking. Yet another rogue hair to extract
You moisturise, apply fake tan, paint fingers, toes and face
Wonder if tonight's the night that you'll let them get past first base
      (And then get clean sheets out of the cupboard, just in case)

Role number 5 is different for us all, but many Mum's have a career
Well, we've got plenty of time on our hands. Sorry, did I not make that clear?
Doctor, Lawyer, Marketing Manager, Designer, Nurse, even Police
Some used to work in the City, now they're busy spending their redundancies
You try to act professional but you can't get Bob the Builder out of your head
You miss the kids terribly.... but it's that nursery phone call you dread
Lunchtime signals a change of role, but what will it be today?
Head Domestic needs milk and bread, but Amelia owes 3 kids play
      (While Event Co-ordinator screams "Harry's party is only 3 days away!")

So there you have it; multi-taskers. What an amazing act we perform
But there's something else... something loud & small. Okay, now we're getting warm
Illogical and time wasting; sometimes too clever, often too dumb
How could we forget Role Number 6? Of course we're a full time Mum!

Bloomin' Bump

Pregnancy probably deserves a book to itself; there are so many moans to list
But hopefully a page and a half of ranting will give you the general gist
Morning sickness, sciatica, those strange skin complaints
The need to eat 2 hourly or otherwise you'll faint
 Hot flushes, the need to pee, can't stay awake past nine
Thumps and kicks in the middle of the night, just to show Mummy they're fine
Constipation, indigestion, stretch marks a daily surprise
And all that without mentioning, your sheer bloody size

First time round, let's be honest, you're quite content with all that I mention
"No pain, no gain" registers somewhere, and besides you get a lot of attention
Long afternoons eating Krispy Kreme Doughnuts while curled up on the sofa
Almost makes up for the lack of alcohol and being everybody else's chauffeur

You strip the shelves of baby magazines, way too tired to read a book
You hungrily digest every word, amazed at how the baby will look
   (And if they're 2 inches, why has your midriff grown by a foot?)
At work you log onto ivillage, read about childbirth, and then regret it
Do they not realise how emotional you are? Surely those stories should be vetted?
In the second trimester you're feeling better so tackle Contented Baby by Gina Ford
You like the idea of them sleeping through early, but the routine seems a little flawed
   (i.e. "Having a life" seems to have been ignored)

You have a constant battle with yourself over what food should pass your lips
In the beginning you can't stomach anything, except a plate of salted chips
You know it should be nuts and seeds, green vegetables and plenty of water
But your baby seems to prefer Chocolate and Flapjack, blame it on having a daughter
And then there are all the foods you can't eat, from soft cheeses to tuna steak
Does feta count? Can I eat prawns? None of these problems with Banana cake...

You buy the book of ten thousand names, then realise it's all a bit pointless
You already know hundreds of them, what's tricky is getting a consensus
"Amelia, Sophie, Isabella, Katie!" they shout with desperation
"Lola is far too racy and Luby is just your creation"
"Boys should have solid names. William, Edward or Tom
If we call him Luca, where will people think we're from?
Your urge of course is to argue back, regale all his name's flaws
But you're quietly confident, after hours of pain, the decision will be yours

At 7 months, husband in firm grip, you arrive at your first NCT meeting
He had suggested you attend the Mum's only class, but you tell him that would be
     cheating
You look at the other oversized ladies and quickly start to bond
It's the petrified and unprepared look in their eyes to which you're instantly fond
Together you listen to your NCT teacher talk about the beauty of natural labour
So it's strange that an epidural seems to be something you naturally favour
You start to think that maybe they're right and set about writing your birth plan
Then you watch the video. Husband sweats. Asks for water and a fan
"It's a hard decision" you tell the girls "but on reflection"
"Natural childbirth isn't for me", and book in for a caesarean section

Travkelling

You know that lady on the aeroplane, the one with the secret smile
Peacefully flicking through her magazine, giving her nails a leisurely file
She's not perturbed when the plane's delayed; in fact her smile seems to grow
She adjusts her headphones, plumps her pillow and exchanges OK! for Hello
But on departing she can't resist the "double check" and thus her cover is blown
No wonder she is basking in serenity, she's a Mum who's left her kids at home

Because travelling with kids is always a challenge, whatever mode of transport you take
Be it car, bus, plane or train, a troublesome journey they'll make
From throwing a tantrum to refusing to walk, to running right out of sight
Over tired with a sugar rush, and then confined on a 4 hour flight
Parental ineffectiveness is at its most obvious, the learning curve far too steep
Infact the only chance of pain-free travel is to do it when they're asleep

Our most regular form of transportation is travelling in the family car
Kids strapped in, vaguely out of sight, nice if you don't have to go too far
But soon the whinging is underway and the infamous "how long 'til we get there?"
You wonder how many Princess Poppy book CDs the rest of you can bear
"I spy, something blue!" "My top? Harry's shoe? The sky?"
"That's right! Now your turn Mummy!" But 3 hours on, you're ready to cry
Luckily you've come prepared, can meet any food request
Dried apples? Fresh strawberries? But Iced Gems or Quavers are best
You suggest they pass the time with a nap, but "we're not tired!" they scoff
Until you're moments from your destination and then it's "Bugger, they've nodded off"

Perhaps you choose to travel by train, make the journey an adventure
You explain, in the interests of safety, some of their behaviour you'll have to censor
"Stay close to me, hold my hand when I say, and NEVER cross the yellow line"
You've only got as far as Clapham Junction and you already need a glass of wine
Dozens of men pretend not to notice as you try to bounce up the Phil & Ted
Concentrate on one task for too long and it's "Okay, where the hell is Fred?"
The journey itself is not too bad, their excitement quite contagious
But disembarking with bags, buggy, kids and latte can be rather dangerous

From time to time we go further afield, which sometimes involves a plane
Excitement starts when the tickets are booked and never appears to wane
You often leave in the early hours, so try to keep the kids asleep
Eyes snap open, they leap out of bed. Adult conversation will have to keep
They run amok in the car park as you try to unload the bags
They test out the trolley's scootering skills while you frantically write the tags
They demand to sit on the check-in desk, give the lady their own passport
She thinks they're adorable, because her time with them is short
Emily refuses to go in the buggy, ride on Trunki or choose to walk
You consider leaving her in the airport but the security guard's watching you like a hawk
 (And anyway, her brother is bound to talk)

You finally make it on to the plane, but there's still a 3 hour flight to go
The couple behind you are travelling kid free, and their concern is starting to show
 (An emotion that is only set to grow)
Emily wants the window seat while Tom wants to race down the aisle
Barges into the air stewardess, which dissolves her painted on smile
Buttons are pressed, tray goes up and down, and husband spies an empty seat
"Leave me now" you whisper gently "and that's 3 days in a health retreat"
But as the sun shines on you when you depart, you wonder what's all the fuss?
Until you realise with growing horror, there's still 3 hours on a charter bus

You feel travelling should teach your children new skills, like developing their imagination
Amusing themselves, the art of time keeping and of course the need to be patient
But the reality is quite far removed; they just run around creating chaos
So forget the lessons in social development and invest in a few DVD players

Laughter lines? Hilarious...

We love our children, of course we do, infact we're slightly addicted to having more
But that doesn't detract from the unfortunate truth, motherhood carries one serious flaw
They may keep us young with their funny comments, the truth when a lie would do
Help us find humour in simple things like bottoms, willies and poo
The may remind us Sunday includes a morning, or force us to get active in the park
But they can't hide the accelerated march of the years, as those circles become a new
    shade of dark

They can't stop the spread of varicose veins, reaching out like the roots of a tree
Or the stretch marks that extend from tummy to bottom, never again to wear a bikini
They can't stop the way my boobs shrink and sag, my nipples turned to well worn leather
Or the fact my belly hangs over my jeans, those abdominals never quite stitched together
    (But my, aren't those big pants so clever??)
They can't stop the way my back aches every day, carrying a 2 stone child
Or the calluses that have appeared on my feet, no matter how regularly I've filed
They can't stop my teeth from wasting away, from filing to root canal to crown
Or the way my forehead appears stuck, with an ever deepening frown
But most importantly, above all else, they can't give me back my skin
The glowing look of youth and rest is now lost in the proverbial bin

Men are jealous of their kids when they're older, when they beat them at tennis or squash
When they introduce them to their gorgeous girlfriend or start to earn some serious dosh
But Mum's are jealous of their babies, is that an okay thing to admit?
If I promise to do it under the protective haven of rhyme and a little wit?
We're jealous of their perfect skin, not a freckle, not a mole, not a line!
Its elasticity a sight to behold, bouncing back in record time
No "laughter lines" or "crow's feet" or worry etched with a permanent indent
We used to have skin like that, before we decided to become pregnant

Hormones, sleepless nights, pregnancy, labour and stitches
Breastfeeding, post baby blues, the routine of routine glitches
Comfort eating, comfort drinking, hiding your stress with a smile
Multitasking, no OFF switch, the responsibility of raising a child
Burning the candle at both ends, lie-ins a fading dream
These are the things that force us to spend a fortune on miracle cream

From Eve Lom to Dr Brandt, Clarins to Clinque to Nuxe
You try Olay and No 7, hoping those write-ups weren't just flukes
Laura Mercier, Origins, By Terry (By Golly the price!)
Is it really going to work for me because it's been a success for mice?
L'Oreal, Dr Haushka, Revive, Lancome and Ren
All these creams to help me return to the elusive "way back when"

Not satisfied with hundred pound creams, we frequent a Spa when we can
For facials, seaweed wraps, mud floatation, and a St Tropez tan
  (In fact, a perfect getaway if it wasn't for the alcohol ban)
We drink gallons of water, do our best with green tea, and choose muesli made by
    Rude Health
We immerse our diet in essential fats, although flax seeds seem to stay on the shelf
We try supplements, celebrity secrets, juice from the Mangosteen rind
Goji berries, soya beans, and any other superfoods we can find
We lather our face in avocado, rest lemon slices on our eyes
Skin doesn't appear younger, but window cleaner gets a surprise

But just as you start to look a little fresher, your skin find a bit of a glow
You're invited out for a boozy girl's night, and who are you to say No?
Three bottles of wine and as many hours sleep, and it's back to that dreary Square One
A grey pallor engulfs your skin, radiance writes its own Dear John
But is there a way you can have it all, young looking skin and have a laugh?
Of course – you just need Collagen injections and 2 weeks on the Algarve

Slave (to) Labour

The pain of childbirth is quickly forgotten, downgraded to "obscure nightmare"
Enabling us to do it again "So, I had a third degree tear, who cares?!"
Yes hormones have a lot to answer for, to block it out so easily
And in turn, mean it's a shock to discover that when we need a wee, we pee, immediately
So I consider it almost a duty to eternalise these stories in rhyme
In the hope that at least one Mum will consider contraception next time
    (Bytheway, names have been changed in case "gross exaggeration" is a crime)

Zoe is a Mum of twins, so number 3 comes in rather a rush
Waters breaking in George's car park causes a bit of a fuss
But nothing compared to the head appearing in the Lanesborough Wing corridor
Zoe finally makes it into the lift as the porter collapses on the floor
    (And the cleaner realises she's got more than she bargained for)

Kate is a festive romantic, although it's something she learns to regret
Contractions coming thick and fast, she's not prepared for the reception she'll get
"Oh love, Christmas conceptions are so popular" says the receptionist with a chuckle
"Better ask him to hold in tight, because bed-wise we've got f**k all!"
10 minutes later, Kate's in an oversized cupboard, delivering baby James
Husband holds her legs back for stitching, while Kate calls him names
    (And resolves that next year she'll stick to more traditional Christmas games)

Anna is a Pilates Instructor; she believes it's all in the breathing
Positive thinking and a glass of Pinot will be sufficiently pain relieving
Anna's not stupid. She knows this approach could be a little tough
So she attends the courses, reads the books. You can't say she's not done enough
So it's a bit of a shame when her first born enters the world at such a pace
Delivered by husband on the kitchen floor is how Anna meets baby Grace
    (Although the bottle of Pinot still disappears without trace)

And let's spare a thought for Marathon Mum, their story less dramatic
But trust me; 3 days of hell can be equally problematic
Gas and air to pethidine, epidural to spinal block
Husband naps in the armchair, while midwife watches the clock
At last you're told it's time to push, thank goodness it will soon be over
You thank the midwife, give her a hug, even though you secretly loath her
But 3 hours later, it's not to be, despite forceps, ventouse and prayer
So you're wheeled down for an emergency section, although by now you really don't care

There's the Mum who got a shock one morning, when she sat on the toilet seat
Slightly put off from doing her wee, at the sight of 2 tiny feet
Or the Mum who thought her water's had broken, but the fluid was more blood red
Ambulance to Chelsea & Westminster who quickly whipped out baby Fred
There's the baby lying breech which meant a C-section for her Mum
Caused quite a scene when the surgeon's scalpel nicked her baby's bum
There's the Mum who wanted an epidural but the anaesthetist was nowhere to be seen
Wicked rumours started to spread that he was on the 18th Green
Or the husband who turned up moments too late, bad traffic his excuse
Wife too knackered to really fight, so she let her mother loose
        (And so started some serious abuse)
There's the Mum that had a homebirth, for pain relief just a spliff
But then I remember this is Wandsworth, so that's probably just an Urban Myth

There is of course the odd Mum who tells her birthing story full of smiles
And while I try to be mature about it, to be honest, it slightly riles
Because if I liken childbirth for a moment to a game of Russian roulette
Then unfortunately for me, I haven't spun an empty barrel yet...

On your marks...

Us Wandsworth Mums are so enlightened, we understand a child's need for space
To develop their skills naturally, at their own (somewhat slow) pace
We don't get embarrassed during Rhyme Time when our child refuses to sing
Or when they can't take part in Playball because they're too busy tantruming
We still love them when they perform ballet, without a hint of grace
Or when they fall and refuse to get up during the egg & spoon race
In fact, our child's ability is something that we never question
And if you see things differently, you've got entirely the wrong impression
   (After all, "2ⁿᵈ place is for losers" is just an expression)

The competitive streak appears early, "Katie's smiling! And she's only 5 days!"
"Well, William saves his smiles for me (if I look directly into his gaze)"
"Chloe slept right through last night, and she's only 8 weeks old!"
"I'm sure it's nothing I've done..." is the smug way the story's told
"Benji is down to 4 feeds now, and he winds in record time"
"Millie doesn't wind at all. Gosh, I'm SO glad she is mine"
You wonder, as you look around, if the other Mums are a tiny bit jealous
Their babies are a bit, well, odd looking, don't have a beautiful face like Bella's
   (A year later, you look back at the photos and realise you were a little over zealous)

Now you have a taste for competition, and you reckon Tommy's in the top five
You secretly pray he'll walk before he's one, just to keep the dream alive
You buy the famous yellow walker; curse that Puppy song for being so loud
But it'll be worth it when Oli takes his first steps, hopefully in front of a crowd
And finally he does. He's walking! Now the world is your oyster
From ball skills to running and jumping, Sam will be a BOY STAR!

And so starts the merry-go-round of every pre-school class around
From Playball to Gymboree, that'll be another hundred pounds
Ruggerbeez, Socatots, Ballet ("No Tommy, that's just for girls")
Gymnastics, Swimming, Tennis, singing at the local church
French classes, Mange Too, Stage Coach for the under fours
Not forgetting 5 mornings of Montessori of course
In fact we go to extreme lengths, and spend a fortune too
To ensure when our children start reception, there's absolutely nothing for them to do

But let us spare a verse for Dads as this is an area in which they excel
Competitive Mums might be hard work, but Competitive Dads are straight from hell
"Come on Frank! Crying is for girls! Get Up! Stick the boot in!
These kids might be here to take part, but you are here to win!"
Or it's "Jemima is my little princess, she has the face of an angel"
Funny, it doesn't seem to bother them that she might also possess a brain cell
So is it true? Do Dads win in this competition for competitiveness?
Or is it that Mums hide their urges behind subtlety and finesse

From Easter bonnets to "Bring a book week" we just can't help ourselves
Finding the perfect fancy dress when Ben's cast as one of the elves
Whispering words of encouragement when they don't want to go to school
Wolf whistling their first swimming strokes from the edge of the pool
Spending hours reciting numbers, when they just want to watch TV
Watching them write their name for the first time with unexposed glee
    (And no, M-A-X isn't particularly easy)

But it's not really competitiveness that drives us to do our best
It's about being thankful for the children that we have been blessed
It's about not closing the door on the potential they have shown us
And if they happen to win the Playball trophy, well that's just an added bonus

Bath ~~wine~~ time

I used to go to the gym to earn it, or find a friend who needed a shoulder
Race to finish a work document, the glass whispering for me to hold her
Perhaps I'd clean the bathroom, paint a room or mow the lawn
Or there could be medicinal reasons, having partied until dawn
Yes, there's plenty of things I've done in my past to merit a glass of wine
But nothing quite so deserving as the challenge of kids bathtime

While we do it every day, it's still the stuff of nightmares
Trying to get all three children up that long flight of stairs
You've already had the hell of teatime, so your resolve isn't strong
You briefly consider giving it a miss, but you know that would be wrong
    (And a slippery slope to having children who rather pong)
You try the racing game "First one to the top is the winner!"
But realise you've worn that thin when Sophie mumbles "such a beginner..."
Next the threat of punishment: "Upstairs NOW or no TV!"
Weirdly no response to that but they'll move to "One... Two... THREE!"

You start to run the bath water while Todd empties in all the toys
Phone rings – husband's running late – but you don't hear it above the noise
"But I don't NEED a wee!" Sophie shouts with genuine indignation
Funnily enough, once manhandled onto the toilet, she rises to the occasion
    (And if you're really unlucky, adds the "actually I need a poo" complication)

Finally you get them into the bath, but the worst is yet to come
Keeping yourself free of a soaking is Priority Number One
"I wanna sit that side!" "No, me!" "No, ME!" they cry
"Mummy don't wash my hair, you'll get shampoo in my eye!"
"That's my duck, not yours! Mummy! Toby's got my DUCK!"
"Gosh, I could pretend I care, but actually I don't give a... monkey's"

You wonder why your son, who refuses to drink more than a sip
Can happily gulp gallons of bathwater every time he takes a dip
From sucking through a flannel to drinking from a mould stained cup
You eventually tell him to stop when you realise he liable to throw it up
Another splash of water gets you, and the air's getting steamy hot
You suddenly remember an "emergency" downstairs and you're off at a trot
News is on TV, so you pause (just a moment) to get the headline
"BABY DROWNS IN 2 INCHES OF WATER" kind of spoils your "me time"

As it was such a struggle to get them in, getting them out should be a synch
But of course it doesn't work like that, the task still seems to require a winch
Still water in the bath, Todd feels his job is far from done
Toby has got all three ducks now so he's having far too much fun
Sophie is happy to get out of the bath but wants to do it all on her OWN
Husband rings again so you bark "I NEED A DRINK!" down the phone

Finally they're all out and it's time to clean their teeth
Which inevitably means for you another intense round of grief
Sophie won't let you run the tap, something she learnt at school
Todd, transfixed by water, regularly likes to break that rule
Toby isn't keen on brushing, but he happily sucks the toothpaste
Well, he's only got 7 teeth, and surely it's a good sign he likes the taste?
    (As you try to forget the amount of chemicals with which it's laced)

Into their pyjamas, ordeal over you realise with a sigh
7pm, the end's in sight and you're on a bit of a high
But then you remember, there's still the torment of 3 x story time
Thank God that only requires one hand, as you pour that glass of wine

Once upon a grime...

Hang on, isn't it the mother who's supposed to be the resourceful one?
Isn't making "something from nothing" an area where we've always shone?
Yes we can make dens from blankets and cushions, or tea from twigs and stones
Sure, we can create music from pots and pans or turn remote controls into phones
We may be able to mould party food from Play Doh, or a puppet from husband's shirt
But we can't compete with our kids in one sphere – the ability to conjure up dirt

We go to a family garden party, cucumber sandwiches on the ancestral doily
Not the environment to get filthy we decide, can we, for once, breathe easy?
  (Then we see Emily up a tree. Skidding down it on her knee...)
Grass stains used to be the bane of our mothers' lives, now of course they are ours
Although nothing compared to Grandpa's wrath when he sees the state of his flowers
You leave the event; adults are clean (except for obligatory spot on husband's tie)
Children say "Guess what's green, brown and ketchup!" as they merrily play 'I Spy'

Another day you decide to go to the park, have fun on the swings and slide
But puddles prove too much of a magnet as the worlds of mud and water collide
Felicity likes to ride through on her bike, so her dirt is limited to splatters
Hugo prefers to wade through them, but his jeans are so old it hardly matters
But Tommy, he wants to roll in puddles, get dirty from head to toe
As you look on with growing horror, you decide the Peppa Pig DVD has to go

Then there's the dirtiness kids create at the infamous meal time
How a simple thing like ketchup can turn your kitchen into a scene of crime
Blonde curls died with pasta sauce, nostrils filled with cheese
Cherub lips framed with Rachel's yoghurt, broccoli sprouting out like trees
Floor, walls, table and chairs, yes our children are messy fans
Except of course on one part of them, then it's "Mummy, my hands, my HANDS!"

There's one area where kids manage to turn the theory of getting dirty on its head
They take the concept of becoming clean, and make a helluva mess instead
And with such a reputation to live up to, it's not something they do by half
Which is why mums suggest protective clothing, when giving your kids a bath
Water, bubbles, shampoo and toothpaste – a cocktail of kid's hygiene
But when they're mixed together with the toilet brush handle, somehow not so clean...

Treasure Chest

Breast is best apparently. I know that, because I read it somewhere
Or was it rammed down my throat so hard there wasn't room for air?
    Ah yes, that was it
To be honest, I feel quite honoured that breast feeding worked for me
Conscious that however hard they try, some Mum's aren't so lucky
So if I had my time again, there's nothing I would change
But it doesn't detract from feeling, well, that it's all a little strange

It's strange that one minute you're watching TV, all relaxed on the sofa
An NSPCC ad comes on, and you're leaking through your pullover
Odd that one minute you're carrying around a pair of proud size E's
A few guzzles later, and you lose two sizes with ease
    (and they're hanging somewhere around your knees)
And let's all admit, having sex during this time is weird
The wrong gland being stimulated is something we've all feared
But in the realms of strangeness, the act of "expressing" is hard to beat
One hand pumping monotonously, the other flicking through a copy of Heat

As if strangeness wasn't enough, there's all that pain to endure
To which the midwife answers helpfully "doing it more is the best cure!"
From let down to latching on, cracked skin to uterine contraction
The challenge, when the door bell goes, of unrequited nipple extraction
The pleasure/ pain of them sleeping through, you're of course wide awake
Rigidly unmoving, boobs could explode with the smallest shake
But while feeding your child with mastitis may hurt beyond belief
It's really just preparing you for the day that your child grows teeth

If it's not oddness or pain to deal with, it's embarrassment instead
Father-in-law entering the feeding scene just as Amber raises her head...
It's the muslin slipping off your shoulder in a busy Pizza Express
Or at your best friend's wedding, the breast pad poking out of your dress
It's burning their head with a Chicken Madras, routine running a little 'lax
Or the midwife noticing how their ears are extraordinarily devoid of wax

There are of course lots of plus points to feeding au naturelle
And that's without being bewitched by the Primary Care Trust spell
No need for sterilising, and the milk's always the perfect heat
Don't have to pay for Aptamil or understand the flow size of your teat
And for those of you who fear that feeding causes breast reduction
Could it also be the socially acceptable alternative to liposuction?

Night Night, Sleep? Might...

And so we turn to an exhausting subject, but one that's close to our hearts
How we now have to take our beauty sleep in quite individual parts
It is with a wistful smile that we remember ambling to bed at eleven
Nothing disturbing our peaceful slumber before the alarm rings at seven
Now we have these little people who like to wake us in the night
It's amazing how, at 3am, your gorgeous child becomes such a ....

Depending on their age, the concern could start by 4pm
They've slept all day, not a good sign, already considering Nurofen
You start with gentle tickling, but end banging Freddie's drum
Thank God for Gina Ford, who considers you a perfect Mum

For older kids there are a hundred reasons why they'll spoil your night
Why you'll hear that voice crying "Mummy!" with Oscar worthy fright
Why, in turn, your husband continues snoring, so unaware of their plight
So you grit your teeth, smile sweetly, and tuck them in EXTRA tight

At 1 we blame it on teething, the "catch-all" for bad behaviour
You herald the magic of Nelson's Teetha, while Calpol is your secret saviour
But as you lift them free of their cot, they're grinning from ear to ear
You want to blame it on excruciating pain, but that diagnosis is becoming less clear
    ("Have you been had by a 1 year old?" you begin to fear...)
After 4 recitations of Twinkle Twinkle don't work, you retreat for a bottle of milk
At least you don't lace it with Medised (this time) so there's really no reason for guilt

At 2 they develop an imagination and you enter the night terrors phase
You can't even bring yourself to be cross as you strip their sweaty PJs
You need to break them out of its spell to ensure the nightmare doesn't repeat
A genuine excuse to raise your voice? Ahhh the moment is sweet
And as you finally stumble back to bed, looking forward to another day wrecked
You wonder if Iggle Piggle drifting out to sea is having the wrong effect

At 3 there's nothing really wrong but they'll wake you all the same
It seems to them that night time stand offs have become a bit of a game
Of course you try to just ignore them, bury your head and keep fingers crossed
But as their shouts wake up number 2, you realise delay brings a heavy cost
    (And if it is a game, you have a sneaking suspicion you just lost)
The good news is, by this age, fulfilling their demands is a piece of cake
    (Largely because they're fake)
However, the bad news, as they fall back to sleep, is you're now wide awake

At 4 you reluctantly decide that the night time nappy has to go
Well, one more comment from Mother-in-law and it could lead to blows
But even though you light the way with Blackpool-esque illumination
They still can't make the 10 foot journey alone. So to Plan B – dehydration
Or even worse, midnight accidents "Mummy! I dun a wee!" they say
You strip the bed in record time, and ignore the obviously damp duvet

Of course even if your kids don't interrupt your beauty sleep
There are a million different reasons why you'll end up counting sheep
Damn, you forgot to buy a present and it's Oli's party tomorrow
And was it the Spiderman suit or Sportacus that Ems needs to borrow?
Book the dentist, collect that parcel and get money out for the cleaner
And it couldn't be true could it, that Isabella punched that sweet Amelia?

And so the magic merry-go-round of motherhood never stops
How apparent that procreation was invented before clocks
The irony of course being how quickly it ages you
With endless broken nights in store, frankly there's little Space NK can do...

Situation vacant: Father (full time)

Some of us like the brainy ones, others prefer Tarzan appeal
Of course career prospects are key, an ex-wife far from ideal
Sometimes we fall for their sense of humour. Everyone likes a laugh
While other times it's what they do under the cover of bubble bath
But then you have children, and suddenly the ONLY way they make you happy
Is by giving you a lie-in now and again, and changing a dirty nappy

In the beginning hormones are raging and you're lost in maternal bliss
So you don't really notice that their parenting skills are at best, rather hit & miss
They love to hold them when they're smiling, or push them sleeping in the Bugaboo
But as soon as they hear a whimper it's "Darling, I think they want you."
They weigh up the pros and cons of breastfeeding, getting behind the idea full throttle
Their wife getting their tits out in public? Obviously preferable to giving the late night
bottle

As time moves on, wrinkles deepen and motherhood loses its sheen
You gently explain over the new Jamie dish, that it doesn't feel much like a team
You point out banana mashed into the carpet is now your idea of a party scene
While they've been on 3 stag weekends, you haven't left SW18
("Arghhh! I'm imprisoned by the routine!")
"How can you say that!" they quickly rebuff "I think I do my fair share!"
"You were gone for ages last weekend and Archie was a bloody nightmare"
"Darling I was in Sainsbury's!" and on you take it from there

You sense that these discussions are making little progress
They continue at "playing" Daddy, while you clear up the mess
So you opt for extreme measures because, without wanting to sound too blunt,
Why the hell should they have a life, when yours is nonexistent?
And then the idea strikes, suddenly you know exactly what to do
A valid reason to get them more involved, even from their point of view
Although it does of course have a fair few repercussions for you
But you still invest in designer knickers – it's time for number 2!

As a family of four, you find they semi throw the towel in
Although they still seem to disappear when both kids are howlin'
You come to terms with the fact that there are some things they'll never do
Plan, organise, pack a bag, find Sophie's missing shoe
They'll never tidy away the toys, or check for dirty feet
And is it me, or do Dad's not realise kids need to eat?

But in the main, they approach their role considerably more robustly
We smile at first, not quite realising quite how much this will cost me
"Three hours in the hairdressers. Coffee with Becky makes four
I believe a round of golf is owed" as they scurry for the door...
"Hang on! You've had 3 weekends away. I'm surely owed much more?"
"Darling, those points are out of date – and this week, you haven't scored"
    (*Funnily enough, you view this barter system slightly flawed...*)

Lucky for you, there's always a friend whose husband is a saint
"Takes the kids for whole weekends you know" is a picture you like to paint
Lucky for him, there's another friend whose husband doesn't lift a finger
A topic of conversation on which you see no need to linger
But while we moan amongst ourselves, we daren't make too much of a fuss
Well, we can't have THEM making a better parent than US!

But if children seem too much and it really comes to blows
If their constant whinging means that the cracks start to show
If their public meltdowns are just too much to bear
You MUST face up to your problems... and get an au pair

Rainy Sunday

It's 6 o' clock in the morning and your head hurts like hell
Then you hear that dreaded sound: pitter patter on the stairwell
You turn over in bed with a sigh, face the other way
But it's pitter patter that way too, another rainy Sunday

Kids have watched 3 hours of Five and it's only nine o clock
Husband hasn't risen yet, claims he's in a state of shock
    (not those 3 bottles of red then, you mock)
They eat their breakfast at 7, then most of yours at 8
Sam is asking for lunch now, but you tell him he's going to have to wait
Luckily there's one thing that stops you losing your will to live
It's a Kids Thing opens soon, and the temporary reprieve that could give
"Sorry love, we're fully booked. I guess it's all this rain"
"No problem!" you reply merrily, a relaxed approach you've learned to feign
"Okay children, no It's a Kids Thing, so where do you want to go party?"
You're thinking: Gambado's is well placed for lunch, while Eddie Katz does a very good
    latte
"The old Tiger's Eye!" they shout in unison "Yea! That's our very favourite!"
"Great" you respond through gritted teeth, just wishing you didn't have to stay for it

Husband surgically removed from bed, and guided to the car
Kids reel off a list of demands, but you're just hearing Blah, Blah, Blah
You pray for it to be quiet like at Easter or Christmas Eve
But it's a rainy weekend in February and therefore a bit of a squeeze
    (Accurate use of the verb: to heave)
Children need some restraining while you queue for what feels like hours
But you finally let the leash off and they head for the brightly coloured towers
At last husband comes into his own as he offers to find you a drink
Although when he returns with a cappuccino it pushes you to the brink
    (Does the man not think??)

Amelia causes embarrassment when she insists you dance in the disco
At least you're not a famous rugby player, as Will Greenwood turns up for his go
Lunch boxes purchased for the fruit, kids chuck them around the floor
Finally the staff say "it's time you left", so you're at a loose end once more

You might think the activity would keep them quiet, the treat keep them content
But for some reason unbeknown to you, that's not the children you were sent
A DVD keeps their attention for a time, biscuits extend that some more
But by 3 o clock they're past the point, and you're heading back out the door
Rain is now drizzle and ideas running low, you head up to the common
"No Sam, you can't have your bike AND scooter. Stop whinging Mabel, Come On!"

The beauty of your outing is you're not alone, harassed families adorn the park
Parent's shout, children cry, a brown Labrador discharges a bark
You watch your kids fly the aeroplane, you push them on the armchair swing
Help them conquer the monkey bars, even though you get quite a kicking
You walk them across the caterpillar, provide extra ballast on the see saw
You catch them at the fireman's pole without it appearing like a chore
But why this sudden enthusiasm? Has your hangover finally improved?
No, but husband has mentioned The County Arms. And their sofas will lift any mood
     (and of course they serve kids food...)

Clothes not Clones!

Because we're intelligent, well-informed Mums, we understand the importance of "being
   you"
Of developing a unique personality, having your own point of view
So we encourage our children to be different, to stand out from the crowd
We tell them individuality is something for which to be proud
And then we go to our wardrobe, finger our clothes all neatly hung
And choose designer jeans, Converse and Aviators. After all, we're a London Mum

The park uniform has strict guidelines, particularly when it's cold
An unbranded Mum gets sideways glances, she doesn't fit the mould
Converse, 7's, A&F hoodie, GAP puffer, preferably in white
Scarf wrapped thrice and fluffy gloves, but the woolly hat is just not right
In summer we swap Converse for Hav's, designer jeans for designer short jeans
We consider trying out the legging craze, but their tightness seems a little extreme
Sometimes we choose a denim mini-skirt, when we're feeling reckless
But concerned about our 30 something legs, we accessorise with a brightly coloured
   necklace
   (although hope rises when a builder shouts "Check this!")

For the more formal event like play dates or coffee, we amend our attire of course
Skinny jeans and knee high boots, both shoe horned on with some force
A cashmere wrap completes the look, plus of course those jewels
An SW Mum without an eternity ring is nothing short of cruel
There's cosmetic jewellery from Oliver Bonas, or bought at those Christmas parties
Back then you thought it was festive fun, although William seems convinced they're
   Smarties

It's quite surprising we all look the same, because our shopping options are extensive
As at home in Southside's Primark as we are in Bellevue's more expensive
Northcote Rd unearths the "surf chick" in us, Kings Rd brings out our "rich side"
Top Shop suggests we're in denial about our age, Gap says at least we've tried
Kew is good when you're feeling grown up, Matches if you've got a wedding
Underwear is generally M&S, or Agent Provocateur if husband's been meddling
Shoes we get from LK Bennett but Faith is not off limits
Office is always worth a look, can pick up a new pair of ballet pumps in minutes
Kingston, Richmond, Clapham Junction, Westfield or Oxford Street
Practical needs, a specific outfit or more often just a treat
Because shopping is our passion, if we could, we'd do it day and night
And if we tend to look similar now and again, it only shows we're doing it right

Jeans JEANS! Thank you Lord Fashion, for making them okay to wear
Our Mums with 2 kids and an expanding bottom? Well, they wouldn't dare
But in the 21st century we wear them with love, because they keep the dream alive
Our faces might show the passage of years, but our legs still look 25
Boot, Flare, Skinny and Straight, more cuts than a piece of beef
Dark, Dyed, Distressed and Faded, so many washes it beggars belief
But labels, that's when the choice really starts, which designer is right for me?
Seven, Citizens, Rock & Republic, True Religion, James or Lee?
Earl, Hudson, Paper Denim Cloth, Joe's, Paige or Diesel?
Just a shame with that price tag, having them all isn't feasible

But let's not forget bags, one for every occasion, yes bags come in equal first
From an Anya Hindmarch "I'm not a plastic" to a sleek Prada purse
A Cath Kidson tote bag, Burberry for luggage, or splash out on a Louis Vuitton
It may be purchased in Bangkok, but no one else needs to know it's a con
There's Marc by Marc Jacobs, Chloe, Fendi, Mui Mui or Jimmy Choo
But trying to persuade husband to spend thousands, can be a tricky thing to do
        (especially when Jemima will no doubt cover it in glue)
So we make do with bags from the High St, or a new designer with a future
After all we're south of the river, we don't demand haute couture

As Mum's we're also women of course, and a woman's work is never done
We might be looking fabulous, but we no longer just shop for one
We have our children to style to perfection, so again we think outside the box
And dress them in Jack Wills and mini-Boden, accessorised with Crocs

Mini-Break

However much we love our children, looking after them is rather hard work
Trying to bring them up properly, while pandering to their every quirk
There are also the trials of living in London, from police sirens to white van drivers
Constant traffic congesting the roads, and the oxygen with which they deprive us
So it's not surprising by the summer months, we're keen to get away
To leave behind the stresses of life and find some sunshine we pray
We're not overly concerned by the question of how we're going to pay
It is after all a necessity, for London Mum's to have a holiday

But once you are a family, holidays take some careful planning
To ensure there's enough time to top up levels of alcohol and tanning
Because if you're not too careful you could end up in deepest Lincolnshire
In a remote cottage in a place advertised as Village of the Year
    (Unfortunately which decade they don't make clear...)
No toys, completely un-child-proofed, hosted by a retiree called Clive
You tentatively ask for CBeebies, but he explains they're still waiting for Channel 5
The cottage is a little pokey; thank goodness the garden's too vast to measure
Just a shame England's East Coast isn't known for its balmy weather...

Some of us are lucky enough to have parents with pads on the Coast
Even better when free childcare is thrown in by the host
Whether it's a Mediterranean villa or a cottage in England's South West
Since having the ~~millstone~~ joy of a family, you've become a very frequent guest
    (After all, FOC is always best)
However, negotiating peak week stays can be a sibling nightmare
So much for that parental advice: "Children, it's nice to share"

For others we consider going away with friends, the idea of safety in numbers
But we need to pick who carefully, the potential high for social blunders
Kids the same age, less naughty than ours and definitely no early risers
The longer we've known them the better all round, less chance they'll surprise us
Adults must drink, not tan too well, and certainly no size 8's
Not too keen on the energetic types, or any other equally annoying traits
But when you've ruled out all these people, there aren't many possibilities that leaves
And unfortunately the only family that fits the bill has just booked 2 weeks in the Maldives
    (Either that or Milton Keynes)

For the more adventurous (read: on a budget) there's camping on the Cote d'Azur
Although a permanent structure and air-con means the experience isn't pure
But as we hand-wash in the sink each night or pine for our dust buster
As we search for familiar foods in the supermarket while husband begins to fluster
As we take them on the waterslide yet again or get pushed into the pool
We wonder if so looking forward to this trip suggests we're a bit of a fool
But the sun shines in the sky each day and you have nowhere to be by nine
Sand, water and the promise of ice cream means the kids behave most of the time
And while time on your own may be fleeting, its rarity makes it dear
And if things really start to go awry, there are always those little bottles of beer

But sometimes you deserve a proper break, one that follows the tradition of holiday
Remember that? The concept of stop work, now start play?
A period of time without your hands in the sink, mind planning tomorrow's tea
To spend time with people who when you say "Shall we go?" just simply agree
Time to do the things you used to do, from the crazy to the plain old lazy
Enjoy every night to the max (you think – the memory is a little hazy)
So hang the expense, time to book Mark Warner, full time childcare of course
But something stops you from making the booking, is it the £8k filling you with remorse?
Don't be silly, it's worth every penny, and it's not your money after all
But the nanny's said she'll stay home with the kids, so you're off luxury trekking in Nepal

Tapoo?

There are many ironies of parenthood; Father Christmas is a great example
Such a wondrous tale of make believe, a greater lie we can't pull
You must NEVER cross when the Red Man's flashing (unless you're running
    REALLY late)
Chocolate is only for special occasions (as you try to hide your Flake)
But up there with the biggest ironies is when your child inevitably shouts POO POO!
"Darling, we don't like to mention that word" But that isn't strictly true

The interesting thing about poo is that it has a development all of its own
Newborns may look sweet and innocent, but their cover is quickly blown
Meconium! Someone up there obviously thinks that's a funny trick to pull
New Mums tasked with the challenge of removing tar with cotton wool
And is it me, or is the sheer amount they excrete quite frightening?
And then lo and behold! Black turns to yellow. No wonder poo is so exciting

The noise of babies' pooing means they can never expel with grace
For breastfeeding Mum's there's the "guess what I ate poo", curry comes at quite a pace
Some babies are creatures of habit, poo every day at half past nine
Others choose to save it for those most inappropriate times
    (And usually when they're dressed up to the nines)
And there are those times when you THINK they're finished, their nether regions
    laid bare
The outcome of that is quite disgusting, but it's still a story you like to share

Nothing can prepare you for the change in poo when you start to wean
You fight the urge to leave Timmy on the doorstep with cries of "Unclean, unclean!"
    *(Instead you go for the double nappy bagging, you'll save next year for "going
    green")*
Add a bout of teething or an experiment with homemade quiche
And a face mask is the only answer, plus the urge to wash your hands in bleach
For some babies the change to dairy can bring a period of constipation
The poo finally arrives, after gallons of prune juice, to cries of jubilation
    (As another rabbit dropping rolls off the changing station)

Some children use their poo as a tool, to get their Mum's attention
You smell something suspicious at first light, so enter their room with apprehension
Down the walls and up their arms, the delights of toddler poo smearing
You don't remember THAT in the job description when you took on the role of child
    rearing
With hindsight, this is probably a stage on which your child would prefer you to stay stum
But when you're drinking lattes with your peers, that's just not possible for a Mum

Finally the time you've been dreading arrives, you must potty train your child
Discovering a poo behind the sofa suggests the transition could take a while
But even when they hit the mark, cleaning a potty can be worse than a nappy
You decide only when they progress to the toilet can you be truly happy
But then it's "Mummy, I dun a poo, can you come and wipe my bottom?"
Either that or they use their knickers, you arrive just too late to stop 'em
You wonder with desperation when they'll take responsibility for their own hygiene
You can't imagine a time when they'll care if their bottom is actually clean
    (And if it's a son – it's unlikely to happen before he's 18)

So it really remains a mystery to me why we talk about poo so much
Perhaps it's a way of cleansing ourselves from the filth of what we have to touch
Because there isn't much that's more disgusting than manhandling a child's poo
Except, that is, if you discover that child doesn't belong to you...

More common than you think

Oh darling, mother says every now and then, don't you think it's time to move?
You've been in London 10 years now; you really have nothing to prove
Shouldn't the children be shielded from all these fumes and city dirt?
You grew up in the great English countryside, and it certainly didn't hurt
Just think of what life could be like, all those green open spaces
So you say, "C'mon Mum, I'll take you to some places"

First you take her to Wandsworth Common, our peaceful haven (next to the prison)
It may not quite be rolling hills, but inner city sprawl it definitely isn't
Fresh faced school boys play cricket on the lawn, while babies cause a noise with a drum
A Labrador escapes onto the bowling green while a blonde calls "Common Ground
       Anyone?"
At weekends men take over the common, from tennis to football to childcare
But to see a man on a weekday? Well, we do our best not to stop and stare
       (Particularly if it's Mark Owen who provides A-list celebrity flair)
The playground offers a haven for kids, well at least for the first half hour
Then it's playing made up games in the trees, only injury turning them sour
 Kids learn to ride their bikes on the pathways, dogs weave through to test their skill
They duck under the bars over the railway line, determined to make it over the hill
Tom scoots at speed round the lake decking, but the heron won't be moved from his perch
You're generally still in the Common Ground, so this involves a bit of a search
Fun is had trying the exercise bars, or watching a Personal Trainer
You tell Lucy to stop staring at his chest, but in truth you can hardly blame her
Tired Mums push their babies to sleep, find chance for a girly chat
Toddlers scream and run from their nannies. What's Filipino for "Oi, stop that!"?
At weekends peace is hard to find, once the dawn buggy pushers have gone back to bed
The click clack of studs on the concrete paths drowns out the planes flying overhead
Bank holidays are particularly busy, not put off by the forecast of rain
We don our Hunters and Barbers; another picnic for the Wandsworth insane
But the ice cream van is strategically placed, on route to Belle Vue boutiques
And, you've put up with country living all morning. It must be time for some Mummy treats.

Next you take her to Battersea Park, and you can tell she's starting to fold
With a zoo, gardens, playgrounds and river, suddenly her comments seem a little bold
You get lost in the many garden walkways; get wooshed by a group on blades
You tell women how beautiful their children are, then realise they're just the maids
You spend hours watching the children circle the Pagoda on their bikes
And then you go to pay for your parking. Oh crikes...

If that's not enough, you head to Clapham Common, only 200 acres of green open space
By this point mother has realised she's got some severe egg on her face
Mums still abound during the early hours, but there's another type that visits here
That strange notion of single 20 something, a breed we instinctively fear
Concerts may be worth steering clear off, if only for the thought "what if..."
(And the likelihood that Oli will befriend someone rolling a spliff)

So you head back to Nappy Valley and into SW19
Wimbledon Park has got 20 tennis courts and look, 10 of them are green!
While the South Africans may rule in the evenings, the daytimes are run by the kids
There is never a moment when you don't have a huge gaggle of them in your midst
Whether it's teenagers sailing on the lake, or children feeding bread to the ducks
Whether it's toddlers destroying the sandpit, emptying its contents into their trucks
It could be kids doing Playball or tennis, balls flying through the air
Or stripping off to their nappies, the water chutes spraying everywhere
They're on the monkey bars, off again (oww) or hurtling down the slide
They sit frustrated on the "big girl swings". Well, at least they've tried
The cafe is run by Italians so the coffee is as good as the pasta
The ramp provides good entertainment, and sporadically the odd disaster

While we're here, there's Wimbledon & Putney Commons, have you got time for another
        400 acres?
Or Cannizaro Park with its stunning gardens, are you sure I don't have any takers?
There's Wandsworth Park, situated in Putney of course, which rolls down to the Thames
The cafe there does exceptional cakes, while the kids are off building dens
Perhaps we could head to Richmond Common, we haven't seen any deer
Or Bushey Park near Teddington, that's not far if the traffic is clear
But no, Mum looks tired. And to your point she's not entirely immune
So it's a shame that you're going to have to tell her: you're moving to Singapore in June

Grass greener? Or just grass?

There are many reasons we ponder moving out, from practical to the emotional draw
Bigger garden, utility room and that elusive Bedroom 4
    (That's big enough to swing a cat WITHOUT injuring its paw)
Bike rides down country lanes, sipping homemade lemonade
Church fetes with cream teas, quaint schools, hair in braids
But then you worry: Will I fit in? And so swings back the pendulum
Perhaps more soya latte and Keane, than Jam & Jerusalem?

"Right, that's it" you declare one day "I've decided we're moving out
London may have served us well, but now we have the kids to think about
We need a garden for them to roam in, a vegetable patch for healthy meals
A school that actually has places and, dare I say it, playing fields
I want a utility to hide the washing, a play room to hide the toys
A room where only adults go, oak doors to keep out the noise
We need fresher air to breathe; you know Sophie has borderline asthma
A garage for all your rubbish, a wall big enough to hang your plasma"

The next day and it's "I love living here. It's so perfect for young children
With 3 playzones and 5 parks to walk to, who needs a big garden?
I'm not sure the country is that healthy; to get anywhere you need a car
And village pubs might be cosy, but sometimes you need a bar
I just can't leave my friends right now. They're the only ones who recognise
When I say I want to sell the kids it's just a pack of lies
    (And never a surprise)
Does Ocado deliver nationwide and where would I find Thai aubergines?
That's it, decision made then. The kids will be fine until their teens"

"Oh no! I can't believe it! Charlotte's moving to Cookham Dean
She's just shown me the brochure; it's the prettiest house I've ever seen."
"Tim & Susie go away this weekend" you declare with a heavy sigh
Romantic break, they're calling it. I bet they're house hunting on the sly
Sarah's moved to Sevenoaks, Alex mentioned KFH
What's the point of staying when I won't have any mates?
So that's it, we're definitely going. Don't you try to change my mind
I'll start the research (Google Maps). You pour me a glass of wine."

Hampshire, Surrey, Berkshire, Kent. All Home Counties duly considered
You're vaguely aware there's a few more, but in your world they've never figured
Family drives out to the country, viewing houses you can't afford
You lost in Cath Kidson heaven, the kids somewhat bored
You scrutinise the Ofsted website, decided they're a bit left wing
SATs results and sports facilities are perhaps more your type of thing
Husband digests train timetables, plans his daily commute
Suggests working from home a little, his Boss thinks that's cute
     (And then refutes)
You whisper "pony" in Sophie's ear, so she can't wait to move
The promise of a Wii for Max, ensures the transition will be smooth

So you're finally ready to pack your bags and start your life afresh
But hang on; you're still in London, immersed in open plan living mess
What happened? Is your cluttered house one that no one wants to buy?
But no. You've just heard the news. Sophie's got a scholarship to Wimbledon High

Nativity Festivity

Hallelujah! I've discovered something that having kids actually improves!
A day that's more rewarding for being in the family groove
Perhaps less so in the run up, the spoilt kid syndrome "I WANT THAT"
Or when they stickily finger all the presents as you're frantically trying to wrap
And not so much on those essential nights out, paying for someone to baby sit
Or the next day looking after them, when you're feeling a little bit... under the weather
But on the day? What a joy! Their smiling, excited faces
That is, until Henry works out his present pile is smaller than Grace's...

Christmas starts early when you have kids, round about when they air the first advert
"Mummy, look at that TRUCK Mummy LOOK! It even comes with its own DIRT!"
"Well, you'll have to ask Santa Claus won't you", you say with a (temporary) smug look
Until you remember he doesn't actually exist, and it's coming out of your cheque book
But you try to use it to your advantage: "Well, you need to be GOOD to get what you wish"
The good news is they believe you, the bad news: they have the memory of a goldfish

Nursery does its bit to suggest Christmas is actually in November
Something to do with them breaking up in the first week of December
They practise their carols with unexpected vigour; their voices warm your heart
Camera battery is all charged up; you can't wait for the concert to start
But alas Grace isn't forthcoming, despite your stern words of encouragement
By the interval she's on your knee, and husband's returned to work with a grunt
But she does create you wonderful things: cards, calendar, tree angel
Although helping her write "Luv Grace" on 30 cards can be a little painful

Christmas holidays aren't too bad, as long as you do your shopping in advance
Surviving Kingston at Christmas with 3 kids? Hmmm not a chance....
You do play dates with pass the parcel, musical statues and a treasure hunt
Chocolate is consumed at least once an hour, but the odd Satsuma gives a healthy front
Husband brings home an 8 foot tree; you remind him your living room is only 12 foot square
Kids decorate the 3 branches they can reach, the rest destined to stay bare
The pinnacle of their excitement is Bocketts Farm, a visit to Santa's grotto
While yours is the nursery Mum's night out, where you proceed to get rather blotto

When you've got kids, parents fighting over your attendance reaches fever pitch
You suggest fairness might be to go to neither, but then both Mums call you a bitch
So you decide to spend it all together, who cares if someone needs to sleep on the floor?
Although husband grumbles "It won't be me" and books a room at the hotel next door.
The day of travel arrives at last, and you attempt to pack the car
But you quickly decide the Baby Annabel pram wasn't designed to travel that far
You plan, shove, repack and squeeze, but it's just not fitting in
Husband's present will have to stay behind, well, rollerblades was rather a whim

'Twas the night before Christmas, not a creature was stirring, except of course for your 3 kids
You've told them Father Christmas won't visit 'til they sleep, but you appear to have anarchy in your midst
The noise levels have reached an unfortunate high, not helped by the presence of cousins
And of course the amount of sugar rushing through them, Celebrations consumed in their dozens
You know you really should be stern at this point, but you've lost the inclination
So you stick them in the back room in front of Polar Express, and call it "being patient"
But when you amble up to bed at midnight, a little worse for wear
You're rather surprised to discover them all, fast asleep in Granny's sewing chair

It's half past five in the morning, when you hear that horrifying noise
You stare at the door, claws ready, with that "Go back to bed or else!" poise
But no, it's not you they want as they shout "He's BEEN Granny, he's BEEN!"
So you close your eyes and curl back up, like the cat that's got the cream
But two hours later you start to get curious, actually rather excited too
Well, months of planning have gone into this, and they might even say "thank you"

By half past nine the presents are open, by half past ten you're on the bubbly
By half past one you're on your 2nd bottle and even Uncle Ted is looking cuddly
By half past three, in the nick of time, the host's tear stained face calls "It's ready!"
Turkey, sausages, stuffing and potatoes help you feel a bit more steady
Sprouts, broccoli, carrots and cauli, bring on a little discomfort
Christmas pudding, brandy butter and custard, and you've got a rather distended gut
Someone presents a Christmas quiz, you quickly partner someone clever
A row breaks out when Grandpa can't remember the name of Space Shuttle Endeavour
But when your head is pounding, exhaustion setting in, you just can't stand the noise
You find tranquillity in the company of your children, quietly playing with their new toys

On Northcote we dote

Armies have their HQ, while gangs feel safe on their turf
Sports teams have home grounds, or home breaks if you like to surf
Old men have their locals, city men have their clubs
Cool men have Shoreditch; our men have Youngs pubs
So it's not surprising that SW Mums have somewhere to call their own
A place that we can be confident is filled with just our clones
Sanctity when we're feeling down, a comforting, familiar abode
I couldn't write this book without mentioning the glorious Northcote Rd

As a gaggle of mums we head to Crumpet, vying for buggy space
Oli is back on the road somehow, but Becky has given chase
Tommy has spied the fairy cakes; Molly is stuck on the loo
Amelia is Queen of the castle, Harry needs a poo
Ruby is eating sugar cubes, Marley is under the table
Josh has built a tower with blocks, although it's not looking too stable
But it doesn't matter you smile to each other, because you're behind Crumpet doors
So you drink your coffee, have a chat, and pretend that they're not yours

Another day and you're there with just your kids; it's time for a haircut
Sally's booked up for the next 3 weeks, can't even fit you in when you tut
So you head to Trotters, but struggle to drag them away from driving that car
Unfortunately the fish tank doesn't do the trick, so you bribe them with a chocolate bar
While you're there you can't help having a little mooch around
Which is why husband says "How could 2 haircuts cost one hundred and twenty pounds?!"

Finally you have a morning to yourself, so you head to Questionnaire
You sail through Whistles, and Sweaty Betty, by Kew you just don't care
By White Stuff you're 25, by Fat Face you're in your teens
A mixture of Neal's Yard and Space NK gives you the necessary means
You stop for a Starbucks takeout latte, treat yourself to a blueberry muffin
A friend tells you she can't find a thing, but you're sure she must be bluffing
You walk past Jigsaw, Fat Face Kids, Jo-Jo's and Petit Bateau
Today is me-time you tell yourself, only one place to spend your doe
But then you have a glass of wine or two (well, All Bar One is just so handy)
And you can't keep away from those cute little dresses: to the baby, like candy

Saturday morning with nothing to do, there's no better place to head
Don't know why Boiled Egg & Soldiers closed down, but I think they probably fled
Toddlers throwing tantrums in the street, babies scream for food
Clapham Junction singles stay at home, they don't dare intrude
Organic fruit and veg looks amazing, and is only twice the price
Fresh bread, muffins, pastries and pies means the bread stall is sure to entice
You spend a fortune on Mark Anderson photos; does London ever look that good?
If Northcote Rd committee took over City Hall, well, perhaps it would

You've shopped for your children and yourself, there's only one place left to dress
But of course Northcote Rd knows you well, and so caters with equal finesse
There's Cath Kidson for kitchenware or Rosie's pink bedroom theme
Oliver Bonas for funky extras or Cuisinere for utensils that gleam
There's Doves for your Sunday roasts, Salumeria Napoli for your Italian night
Fara for kids toys, Pretty Pregnant if you get that fright
One Small Step or Trotters means your children will always have shoes
And if you're looking to sell your house? Well, there are a few estate agents to choose

But what is this? The sun is setting and suddenly things start to change
The haven of SW family life is looking a little strange
Buggies replaced with scooter man, lattes replaced with beer
Crying tantrums replaced with pumping music, and then that thing we fear
The thing that ensures we scurry home, why did we leave it so late?
The arrival en masse of twenty-somethings, with freedom in their gait

What if...?

To end this book, a final thought, to consider the question "What if...?"
To step away for a moment from the family life we have chosen to live
What would we be doing right now, if we didn't have kids to entertain?
When would we get emotional, if there weren't children driving us insane?
How would we spend our money, if school fees weren't a concern?
Why would we ever argue without "No, tonight bath time's your TURN!"

The positive that you would still be working is open to some conjecture
But without children holding you back, you'd probably be Managing Director
Yes you'd be working hard, staying late the odd night or two
But you'd have a team of people who might even listen to you
They wouldn't expect unconditional love, or treat you like their slave
They'd woo you with flattery and lattes, their career paths still to pave
You'd rarely get sick of course, without children passing on their bug
But when you did, you'd just pick up the phone, then return to bed all snug
You might work for a company that does duvet days, get paid to stay in bed
And then there are Christmas parties when you're paid to get off your head
Because work of course means salaries, money to call your own
Joyously spent on yet more clothes, until your wardrobe starts to groan

But at work you must hide your mistakes, while Mums can laugh at theirs
And with none of it to call our own, power struggles between us are scarce
Jealousy, lies, underhand tricks, everyone desperate to get to the next rung
Mums consider the day a success when they stop Freddie sticking out his tongue

Evenings are when the fun would really start going out without booking in advance
A Friday night after payday? Hell, let's take a trip to France!
You'd go to the gym when you're feeling sporty, to the pub when you're feeling low
Galleries, restaurants, concerts, wine bars, or you might choose to take in a Show
Cocktails with the girls one night, or an intimate dinner with your other half
A quick drink becomes a big night out when everyone's up for a laugh
But the next morning you're not feeling so great, hangovers getting worse with age
And you're a little concerned that your "Dirty Dancing" caused some peer outrage
You're supposed to be out again tonight, but your body can't take the abuse
You wish you could stay in and watch TV, wish you had a credible excuse...

The weekend would arrive and the world's your oyster, so much "me time" to fill
You might do something exciting, or perhaps you'd choose to chill
Lazy mornings in coffee shops, reading the Times from cover to cover
Or a new sport/ language/ skill to study, your forte yet to discover
You'd pamper yourself with massage and facials, indulgence never off limits
You'd read magazines and invest heavily in face cream, not immune to their gimmicks
But husband's playing golf again and you're not really a pottery maker
You're steering clear of Pip for now, still sore about Nick "the relationship breaker"
So what can you do with all this time on your hands? Time the rest of us yearn?
Well you visit your friends with families, so perhaps there's a lesson to learn...

Holidays of course would bring something special, a reward for all your hard labour
Not concerned with kids clubs or routine, your holidays would have some flavour
There are safaris in East Africa or diving off the Guatemalan coast
Island hopping in the Bahamas, or an Equatorial beach on which to roast
City breaks to Paris or Rome, or a cross Atlantic trip to New York
Whale watching in Reykjavik, back home that causes some talk
Luxury in the Maldive islands, or roughing it in India's Goa
Relaxing in Barbadian chic, or Anguilla if you want things a little slower
There are ski trips to the Rockies, stylish breaks to Marrakesh
Oktoberfest to get us drunk or Champneys to keep us fresh
There are limitless adventures out there, and you'd do them one by one
So does this mean that "life without children" has finally won?

But who would cuddle us when we stubbed our toe, or say "Me luv woo" everyday?
Who would try to carry the shopping or bring their piggy bank to help you pay?
Who would tell you how pretty you looked every time you put on a dress?
Or help you see the funny side of things, when the house is an apocalyptic mess?"
Who would remind us that we're not mortal, or that we should work to live?
That we're lucky compared to so many families, create a desire to give
Who would put life in perspective, when you make a trip to A&E?
Or make you realise that it can be boring to have all time dedicated to "me"
But most of all, who would cause our heart to flip when we tuck them in at night?
So while they can be hard work, all things considered, having children is alright

If you enjoyed reading my poems,
why not follow me on Twitter?
I usually leave a new rhyme every day.

www.twitter.com/Mumrhymes4fun